# Amazing Animals
# Dogs

**Please visit our web site at www.garethstevens.com.**
**For a free catalog describing our list of high-quality books, call 1-800-542-2595 (USA) or 1-800-387-3178 (Canada).**
**Our fax: 1-877-542-2596**

Library of Congress Cataloging-in-Publication Data

Wilsdon, Christina.
    Dogs / by Christina Wilsdon.—U.S. ed.
            p. cm.—(Amazing Animals)
        Originally published: Pleasantville, NY: Reader's Digest Young Families, c2007.
        Includes bibliographical references and index.
        ISBN-10: 0-8368-9095-7   ISBN-13: 978-0-8368-9095-2 (lib. bdg.)
        ISBN-10: 1-4339-2012-3   ISBN-13: 978-1-4339-2012-7 (soft cover)
    1. Dogs—Juvenile literature. I. Title.
    SF426.5.W54 2009
    636.7—dc22                                        2008013377

This edition first published in 2009 by
**Gareth Stevens Publishing**
A Weekly Reader® Company
1 Reader's Digest Road
Pleasantville, NY 10570-7000 USA

This edition copyright © 2009 by Gareth Stevens, Inc. Original edition copyright © 2006 by Reader's Digest Young Families,
Pleasantville, NY 10570

Gareth Stevens Executive Managing Editor: Lisa M. Herrington
Gareth Stevens Creative Director: Lisa Donovan
Gareth Stevens Art Director: Ken Crossland
Gareth Stevens Associate Editor: Amanda Hudson
Gareth Stevens Publisher: Keith Garton

Consultant: Robert E. Budliger (Retired), NY State Department of Environmental Conservation

Photo Credits
Front cover: Dreamstime.com/Tomislav Birtic, Title page: Dreamstime.com/Andra Cerar, Contents page: Anthony Gaudio/Shutterstock Inc., pages
6-7: iStockphoto.com, page 8: Jupiter Images, page 11: iStockphoto.com, page 12: iStockphoto.com/Christer Lassman, pages 14-15: Dreamstime.
com/Daniel, page 16: Anyka/Shutterstock Inc., page 18: Dreamstime.com/Rhonda Odonnell, page 19: Chin Kit Sen/Shutterstock Inc., page 20:
Laila Kazakevica/Shutterstock Inc., pages 22-23: iStockphoto.com/David Brimm, page 24: Dreamstime.com/Dean Bertoncelj, page 26: iStockphoto.
com/Robert Simon, page 27: iStockphoto.com/Barry Ringstead, page 28: Andrew Williams/Shutterstock Inc., pages 30-31: iStockphoto.com/Joe
Gough, page 32 (large): Iztok Noc/Shutterstock Inc. and Dyanmic Graphic, Inc., page 32 (inset): iStockphoto.com/emmanuelle bonzami, page
33: Dreamstime.com/Anke Van Wyk, page 34: Dreamstime.com/Anke Van Wyk, page 35: Merryl McNaughton, page 36 (large): Dreamstime.
com/Fernando Soares, page 36 (inset): Anne Gro Bergersen/Shutterstock Inc., page 37: Norman Chan/Shutterstock Inc., pages 38-39: Dan
Flake/Shutterstock Inc., page 40: Anita Patterson Peppers/Shutterstock Inc., page 42: Dreamstime.com/Iztok Noc, pages 44-45: Dreamstime.com/
Pixbilder, Back cover: iStockphoto.com/Steve Weaver.

Printed in the United States of America

3 4 5 6 7 8 9 13 12 11 10 09

# Amazing Animals
# Dogs

By Christina Wilsdon

**Gareth Stevens**
Publishing

A WEEKLY READER COMPANY

# Contents

## Chapter 1
A Dog Story ...................................... 7

## Chapter 2
The Body of a Dog.............................. 15

## Chapter 3
Dog Behavior .................................... 23

## Chapter 4
Kinds of Dogs.................................... 31

## Chapter 5
Dogs in the World .............................. 39

Glossary ........................................... 44

Show What You Know........................... 46

For More Information........................... 47

Index ............................................... 48

# Chapter 1
# A Dog Story

## The Dog Family

All **breeds** of dogs have a common ancestor—the wolf. Dogs are part of a large family of animals that scientists call *Canidae* (pronounced CAN ih die). This family includes dogs, wolves, foxes, and coyotes.

A baby dog yawned and blinked his eyes. He was cuddled up against his mother, warm and cozy. Soon his brother and sisters began to wake up from their naps too.

The baby dog was three weeks old. At birth, he was completely helpless. His eyes were sealed shut. All he could do was whimper and drink milk made from his mother. But now he could see and hear just fine. He could walk, too—but he was still a bit wobbly.

The baby dog loved to snuggle with his mother. He also liked being picked up by his owner. Sometimes, on warm days, his owner took the baby dog and his family out to the backyard. He loved the fresh air and the feeling of grass on his tummy.

## Puppy Pals

Dogs under a year old are called **puppies** or pups. A group of puppies is called a **litter**. A litter may be as small as one or two puppies or as large as ten—and sometimes more.

When the baby dog was four weeks old, he was ready to explore. He and his **siblings** tumbled out of their "bed box." They tottered across the floor, sniffing. They made puppy growls and bit each other with their tiny teeth. They yipped and whined as they played.

Another week passed. The puppies grew more active. They learned how to run and jump. They tussled and tumbled over each other.

Sometimes the puppies pounced on their mother. When she got tired of being jumped on, she growled at the pups.

The baby dog ran away from his mother when she growled. Then he slid to a stop. What was that thing under the chair? The baby dog grabbed it in his mouth. Then he proudly carried it back to the bed box. He hoped his mother would notice the slipper he had found!

The baby dog began to eat puppy **kibble** when he was six weeks old. He liked the crunchy food. The puppies began to eat more of the kibble and drink less of their mother's milk.

One day some new people came to the house. A girl sat down on the floor with the puppies. The baby dog ran up to the girl. He crawled into her lap and licked her hand. She gave him a hug.

The baby dog's owner picked him up and carried him over to his mother. His mother nuzzled her baby. And then, to the baby dog's surprise, his owner handed him to the girl. He whimpered for his mom—but he also wriggled with joy. He knew he would like living with this new friend.

### A Dog's Life

Many people think that one year of a dog's life is equal to seven years of a human's life. But this isn't really true. Dogs grow at a different rate than humans. A 1-year-old dog is actually like a 14-year-old human. A 2-year-old dog is like a 24-year-old person. A very old dog of 16 years is like an 89-year-old human—not a 112-year-old one!

# Chapter 2
# The Body of a Dog

The puli is a herding dog. Its long ropes of hair look like dreadlocks!

# Dogs in Motion

A dog walks, runs, and jumps on four sturdy legs. Its paws have tough pads and clawed toes.

Some breeds have legs that seem to be a strange size. A basset hound, for example, has short, stumpy legs. These short legs allowed the rabbit-hunting basset to trail its **prey** under low bushes, but not run too fast for the hunters following on foot.

# Waggly Tails

A dog's tail helps it balance as it runs. A dog also uses its tail to **communicate** with other dogs. Some dogs have bushy tails like wolves. Other dogs have long, thin tails or feathery ones. Some dogs' tails curl over their backs. A few breeds are born with very short tails or no tails at all.

# Canine Coats

A dog's fur is called its **coat**. The coat has guard hairs and an undercoat. The long guard hairs keep the dog dry, and the woolly undercoat keeps the dog warm. A dog may have short, medium, or long hair. Some breeds have smooth coats. Some have wiry coats. Poodles are famous for their curly coats.

# Here's to Ears!

Different breeds of dogs have different kinds of ears. Beagles, cocker spaniels, and many other breeds have ears that hang down. German shepherds and huskies have ears that stand straight up.

**Basset Hound**

A dog can hear high-pitched sounds that a human can not. It can also hear sounds from farther away. Many people are amazed when their dog rushes to the door before the family car comes into sight.

# Canine Teeth

Most adult dogs have 42 teeth. Four of these teeth are long, sharp fangs called **canine** teeth. In the wild, a wolf uses fangs to kill its prey. A **domesticated** dog uses its front teeth to nibble food and its back teeth to cut and crunch it. But most dogs seem to gobble up food as if they were still wild animals!

A dog pants to get rid of extra body heat. Panting cools the dog's body just as sweating cools your body.

## A Speedy Animal

The greyhound is the fastest dog in the world. It runs at a speed of more than 40 miles (64 kilometers) an hour.

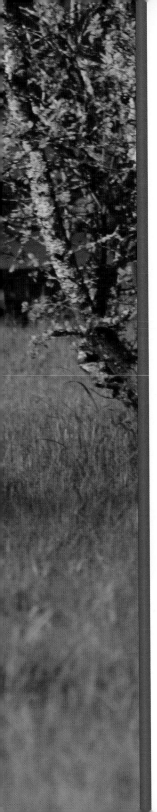

# Sniffing Power

Dogs are famous for their super sense of smell. A dog's nose contains about 220 million cells that detect scents. That's about 40 times more cells than your nose has!

A dog uses its sense of smell more than its other senses to learn about its world. Smelling helps it find food and identify people and other animals.

Some dogs can track down a person even if the trail they are following is two days old. Bloodhounds have followed trails nearly 13 days old.

# Sight Power

Like their wolf ancestors, dogs are good at seeing things that are far away and seeing things that are moving. Both skills are useful for an animal that hunts. Dogs cannot see colors, but they can see better in the dark than you can.

Some breeds of dogs were developed to hunt by sight instead of smell. These breeds are called **sight hounds** or gazehounds. Greyhounds, borzois, and salukis are all sight hounds.

# Chapter 3
# Dog Behavior

Playing games with people or with other dogs is good exercise. It helps a dog stay healthy.

# Family Traits

Dogs are related to wolves, but dogs are domesticated animals. This means they have been specially bred over a very long time to be companions and helpers for humans.

But dogs and wolves still share many **instincts**. Instincts are built-in behaviors and ways of knowing things. Wolves are **predators** that stalk and chase other animals. A hunting dog uses its skill as a predator to track down and catch prey. A herding dog acts like a predator when it chases sheep and steers them in different directions.

# Let's Play

Have you ever been asked to play by a dog? A dog may bring you a toy and set it down at your feet. A dog also says "let's play" by bowing down on its front legs with its hind end in the air. This pose is called a play-bow.

Another favorite doggy game is keep-away. One dog will grab a stick and run with it while the other dog tries to take it away. Keep-away often turns into tug-of-war. Dogs also play these games with people. Wolf cubs play similar games with each other.

# Doggone Fun

Dogs like to chew. This keeps their teeth and gums in good shape. It also keeps them entertained!

Puppies often chew on objects such as shoes when they are growing new teeth. They must be taught the difference between things they can chew and things they can not.

Dogs also like to dig. Some dogs can even burrow under a fence and run off. Many dogs also like to bury bones and other items, just as wolves bury leftover food to hide it from other animals.

Garbage can also attract some dogs. Even well-fed dogs will knock over cans and dig through garbage to find a scrap to eat.

**Dogs spend about 10 hours a day sleeping.**

### Home Alone

Dogs, like wolves, are **pack animals**. They like to be with their family or with other dogs.

Dogs often greet each other with a friendly sniff.

### Dog Talk

Dogs communicate with one another using sounds, body language, and smells. Humans can understand what dogs are "saying" if they pay attention.

# Woofs

Dogs bark to get attention. They bark at strangers, at other dogs, and even at their owners. Dogs also howl. In the wild, a wolf howls to members of its pack that are out of sight. This may be why a dog howls when it is alone. A dog's urge to howl can even be set off by the sound of a car alarm or fire engine!

# Wags

The way a dog holds its tail sends a message to other dogs. A dog holding its tail high is saying, "I'm top dog." A dog holding its tail low is saying, "You're the boss!" A dog with its tail between its legs is signaling fear. An angry dog stares while growling and wagging a stiff tail held high. A friendly dog wags a relaxed tail.

# Sniffs and Whiffs

Dogs learn about other dogs by sniffing them. They also leave scents for other dogs. Male dogs mark trees and objects with urine to let other dogs know they were there. They also mark things where they live in this way, just as wolves mark their territory.

# Chapter 4
# Kinds of Dogs

## Working Dogs

Working dogs include huskies, Great Danes, Saint Bernards, and Akitas. They were bred to help humans and are used as sled dogs, guard dogs, and rescue dogs. A big Saint Bernard can weigh up to 200 pounds (91 kg)!

# Dog Groups

There are more than 400 different kinds, or breeds, of dogs. Dogs that belong to a breed are called **purebreds**. Dogs that are not purebreds are called mixed breeds. Dog breeds are divided into groups by dog clubs in different countries. In the United States, the American Kennel Club divides dogs into seven groups—sporting, working, herding, hound, toy, terrier, and nonsporting.

# Sporting Dogs

The category of sporting dogs includes retrievers, spaniels, setters, and pointers. These dogs are used by hunters to find ducks and other birds.

Labrador retrievers, called labs for short, are one of the most popular breeds in the United States. They can be yellow, black, or brown. Labs make great pets. They're also used as police dogs and as guide dogs for blind people.

**Labrador Retriever**

# Herding Dogs

Herding dogs keep a herd of animals together and move them to different places. They have been used to herd sheep, cattle, reindeer, goats, and even ducks.

Some herding dogs do their job by running around the animals, barking and nipping at their heels. Other breeds even run across the backs of the sheep to get the flock going in the right direction!

# Hounds

Hound dogs were used in the past to track down or chase prey. Some hounds used their noses to track down animals. They were called **scent hounds**. Other breeds used their eyes. They were called sight hounds.

The dachshund is a scent hound. Its short legs and long body let it follow animals right into their underground tunnels and dens.

**Dachshund**

## Just the Right Size

Dogs come in an amazing variety of shapes and sizes. Chihuahuas can be shorter than a cat. Irish wolfhounds can be nearly as tall as a pony!

The Border collie is the best known herding dog. It is famous for moving silently in wide circles to gather its flock.

Dalmatians were once trained to run in front of horse-drawn fire carts, clearing the way for firefighters. Even today Dalmations are often kept as fire station pets.

## Toy Dogs

Toy dogs, often called lapdogs, are small pet dogs. Their only job is to please their owners. Pugs, Yorkshire terriers, and toy fox terriers are a few examples of toys. The smallest dog, the Chihuahua, is in this group.

# Terriers

Terriers, which include Scottish terriers and Jack Russells, are excellent diggers. Just ask a dog owner whose terrier knows how to dig its way under a fence! The name *terrier* comes from the Latin word *terra*, which means "earth."

**Wire Fox Terrier**

Terriers were bred to hunt animals that lived in caves and underground dens. The terrier would wriggle into holes and dig furiously to catch its prey.

# Nonsporting Dogs

The nonsporting dog group includes dogs that do not fit into any of the other six groups—dogs such as chow-chows, bulldogs, Dalmatians, schnauzers, and poodles.

The ancestors of many of these breeds often had jobs to do. Giant schnauzers once herded cattle. Poodles worked as hunting dogs. Chow-chows served as guard dogs and pulled small carts.

# Chapter 5
# Dogs in the World

The dog is often called "man's best friend." It is certainly our oldest friend!

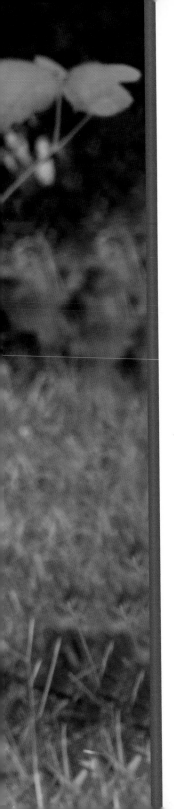

# Dogs and People

People and dogs have been companions for at least 15,000 years. Some scientists think humans may have had dogs even further back in time.

How do we know this? Scientists study canine bones found in ancient human campsites. They also study clues found in the fur and bones of modern dogs.

Nobody knows exactly when a human first tamed a wolf. But we do know that wolves hung around the camps of early humans. They probably ate scraps and other bits of food left behind by the humans.

These early humans may have taken in some wolf cubs as pets. They may have figured out that tame wolves would make useful guards or hunting companions.

# The Domestic Dog

At some point long ago, humans figured out that the tamest, most helpful wolves produced the tamest, most helpful puppies. The humans then paired up, or bred, wolves to get the puppies they liked best. Over time their pets became less like wolves and more like the dogs we know today.

# The Future of Dogs

The world is home to about 500 million dogs. About 60 million of them live in the United States.

Dogs guard buildings, herd sheep, pull sleds, and help hunters. Dogs help people with disabilities by working as guide dogs and service dogs. Search-and-rescue dogs save people's lives. Therapy dogs cheer up patients in hospitals and nursing homes.

Above all, dogs are always ready to be our friends. And most dogs are always ready for a dog biscuit, too!

## Fast Facts About Dogs

| | |
|---|---|
| **Scientific name** | *Canis lupus familiaris* |
| **Class** | Mammalia |
| **Order** | Carnivora |
| **Size** | Up to 39 inches (1 m) tall at the shoulder (Irish wolfhound, Great Dane) |
| **Weight** | Up to 200 pounds (91 kg) |
| **Life span** | From 8 to 16 years (small dogs live longer) |

## The Nose Knows

Here are just a few of the things that people train dogs to find using their super sense of smell: illegal drugs, bombs, land mines, guns, gas leaks, termites, DVDs, cellphones, mold, sea turtle eggs, and brown tree snakes hiding in airplanes!

**Sled dogs can be purebred or mixed-breed dogs. They must be fast and strong and able to pull heavy loads for long distances over a long period of time.**

# Glossary

**breed** — a specific kind of dog

**canines** — long, sharp teeth that are often called fangs. Canines is also another word for dogs.

**communicate** — exchange thoughts, feelings, and information through signs and sounds

**coat** — a dog's fur

**domesticated** — describing animals that have been bred over time to be tame pets

**instincts** — behaviors and knowledge that an animal is born with

**kibble** — small bits of food made especially for an animal to eat

**litter** — a group of puppies born at the same time

**mongrel** — a mixed-breed dog that has parents of different or mixed breeds

**pack animal** — an animal that prefers to live with a group of the same animals

**panting** — a dog's way of cooling off its body by breathing hard and letting its tongue hang out of its mouth

**predator** — an animal that hunts and eats other animals to survive

**prey** — animals that are hunted by other animals for food

**puppy** — a dog that is less than one year old

**purebred** — a dog with parents that are the same breed

**scent hounds** — hounds that use their sense of smell to track other animals

**siblings** — brothers and sisters

**sight hounds** — hounds that use their sense of sight to track other animals

# Dogs: Show What You Know

How much have you learned about dogs? Grab a piece of paper and a pencil and write your answers down.

1. Why does a dog pant?

2. How many teeth do most adult dogs have?

3. Which breed of dog is the fastest?

4. How many different breeds of dogs are there?

5. What emotion is a dog probably feeling if it has its tail between its legs?

6. What were hound dogs used for in the past?

7. Which breed of dog is often kept as a fire station pet?

8. Is the dachshund a scent hound or a sight hound?

9. How many groups of dogs are recognized by the American Kennel Club?

10. Which breed of dog is the smallest?

1. To get rid of excess body heat 2. 42 3. The greyhound 4. More than 400 5. Fear 6. To track down or chase prey. 7. The Dalmation 8. A scent hound 9. 7 10. The Chihuahua

# For More Information

## Books

*A Dog's Best Friend: An Activity Book for Kids and Their Dogs.* Lisa Rosenthal (Chicago Review Press, 1999)

*Everything Dog: What Kids Really Want to Know About Dogs.* Kids' FAQs (series). Marty Crisp (Northwood Press, 2003)

*Puppy Training for Kids.* Sarah Whitehead (Barron's Educational Series, 2001)

## Web Sites

### American Kennel Club: Kids' Corner

*http://www.akc.org/public_education/kids_corner/kidscorner.cfm*

This online newsletter features stories about responsible dog ownership and information about dogs' behavior and bodies.

### ASPCA Animaland Pet Care

*http://www.aspca.org/site/PageServer?pagename=kids_pc_home*

Find out basic facts about dogs and how to care for them. You can also click on a link to watch Pet Care Cartoons.

**Publisher's note to educators and parents**: Our editors have carefully reviewed these Web sites to ensure that they are suitable for children. Many Web sites change frequently, however, and we cannot guarantee that a site's future contents will continue to meet our high standards of quality and educational value. Be advised that children should be closely supervised whenever they access the Internet.

# Index

**A**

American Kennel Club 33

**B**

baby dogs 9–13, 26
barking 29
breeds of dogs 32–37

**C**

chewing 18, 26
communication 17, 25, 28–29, 34–35

**D**

digging 26, 37

**E**

ears 18
eating 13, 18
eyes 9, 21, 34

**F**

fur 17

**G**

group behavior 27
guard dogs 32, 37, 42
guide dogs 33, 42

**H**

hearing 18
herding dogs 16, 25, 34, 35, 37
hounds 34
humans 40–42
hunting dogs 17, 21, 25, 33, 37

**I**

instinct 25, 26

**L**

legs 17, 34
life span 42

**M**

male dogs 29
mother dogs 9–13

**N**

nonsporting dogs 33, 36, 37
nose 21, 34

**P**

panting 19
paws 17
playing 10, 24, 25, 26
police dogs 33, 42

**R**

rescue dogs 32

**S**

scent hounds 21, 34
scent marking 29
service dogs 42
sight hounds 20, 21, 34
size 32, 36, 42
sled dogs 32, 43
sleeping 27
smelling 21, 28–29, 43
sounds 29
speed 20, 43
sporting dogs 33

**T**

tails 17, 29
teeth 10, 18, 26
terriers 37
toy dogs 36
tracking dogs 21

**W**

weight 42
wolves 8, 17-18, 21, 25, 26, 29, 41
working dogs 32